Uncle Amon

WILLY THE WHALE

Short Stories, Jokes, and Games!

Table of Contents

Willy the Whale Discovers His Tale

Willy was a Humpback Whale and he discovered he had two long fins on each side of his body. He waved them and they made him move. When he waved one fin, he moved in the opposite direction. So when he waved his left fin, he moved to the right and when he waved his right fin, he moved to the left.

Willy tried to shake his fins off so he would not be bothered by them, but the more he waved them, the more he moved—in the opposite direction. Finally, he found that when he moved both fins together, they both worked to move him up or down and left or right. After a short while, Willy got used to his fins and he used them to help him move through the water.

The next day, Willy the Whale discovered his tail. He found it on the back end of his body. He didn't know why it was there or what he was supposed to do with it. But the more he tried to get a close look at it, the farther away from seeing it he got.

With a little practice, he found that he was in charge of the tail, meaning he could make the tail stay still or move about. But the more he moved his tail, the more he moved through the water.

When Willy moved his tail while he was looking at it, he moved around and around in circles. First, he looked over his right fin and he turned to the right. When he looked at his tail over his left fin, he moved in a circle to his left.

And when Willy tried moving his tail while he was not looking at it, he discovered that he moved in a straight line. Willy was confused and he was getting angry. He didn't know whether he could trust this tail on the end of his body, but he still needed to learn how to use it.

Now Willy was getting scared. He had two fins and a tail that he had to keep track of so they did not get away from him and so they all did their job. It took Willy a while to learn how to use all three parts together to move where he wanted to go. But once he learned how to make them work together, he could move to the top of the water and breathe fresh air. He could also swim down deep in the water and return without any problems.

Willy discovered that his fins and tail helped him chase after smaller fish at dinner time. And when Willy got too close to big fish, his fins and tail helped him swim back to his mother's side for safety.

Willy was glad to have fins and a tail. He was happy about his different parts because they all helped him move and stop and turn and dive. They helped him find friends and protected him from enemies.

Willy was happy about who he was.

Safety First

Willy is a humpback whale. He and his pod live in the Pacific Ocean. Willy is an adventurous whale and loves to spend time learning new skills and making new friends. Willy's parents do not let him go off on his own, because of the dangers in the water. Even though humpback whales are some of the biggest whales in the ocean, they still need to be careful.

Whales are not fish. They live in the water but they need to breathe air. So when a whale comes up to the surface of the water, he takes a deep breath, and then returns to the water to find food or travel to other places.

The pod was swimming through a deep part of the ocean and Willy wanted to find out how deep the water really was. He came up to the top of the water, took in a deep breath and dove back down, head first. He flipped his tail to help him go down faster and faster.

Willy did not have any kind of meter or machine to tell him how deep he was, so he had to guess. Willy started feeling heavy and slow, but he kept diving.

Willy could almost see the bottom. He did not want to give up, but he was getting tired and needed air. Finally, Willy's mother came up behind him and nudged him upward. "You cannot go any deeper," she said, "or you will die."

Willy was glad his mother was there. He might have tried to dive deeper and he did not know how he would get back to the top. "Mother, why is the ocean so deep if we cannot go all the way to the bottom," Willy asked.

"The water is not made for you," Willy's mother said to her child. "You are made to live in the water and to learn what is good to do and what is dangerous."

"But can't I have any fun in the water, like diving real deep?" he asked.

"You must learn what kind of fun is good and what is dangerous," his mother said.

When Willy and his mother got to the top of the water, they both took a deep breath and spent some time at the top, breathing and playing on the surface. Willy's mother then dove under the surface. Willy dove after her. Willy swam slowly, looking at his mother. Then his mother slowed down even more so that Willy would catch up. When Willy swam just above her tail, she gave her tail a downward flip, which caused Willy to tumble downward.

"Hey," Willy called. He stopped tumbling and started swimming again. He swam up to his mother's head. "That was fun," he said.

"Yes, and it wasn't dangerous," said Willy's mother. "As you grow older and get more experience, you will learn more about what kind of fun you can have without being in danger of getting hurt.

"Thank you, mother," Willy said. He was glad his mother loved him enough to teach him how to have safe fun.

The Pod Moves Forward

As the sun was coming up over the horizon, Willy shook himself awake. He had slept safely between his parents in the middle of their pod, where all the little ones slept. He wanted to swim and stretch and jump out of the water like he had seen the adult whales jump.

Willy bumped into the other whales around him as he stretched. Some of them were young ones and when they awoke, they shook and stretched, bumping against the adults. Eventually, the entire pod awoke and began moving around for the day. They would soon be moving toward food.

Willy joined with three young whales as they swam to the top for air. They blew out the old air through their blowholes and took in deep breaths before submersing again. But this time, each of them went down deep, then turned around and raced for the surface. As they broke through the surface, their bodies kept climbing toward the big blue sky. Willy was still small, so he was able to jump higher than the adult whales. The adults were so big that no matter how hard they tried, they could not jump all the way out of the water, like he had seen the dolphins jump. Dolphins even flipped in the air so they came back into the water tail first. Willy could not do that. Would he ever be able to do that? Or would he get so big that he would no longer be able to leap from the water?

Willy and his friends kept jumping and diving and jumping and diving, each time trying to get higher and higher than the time before. They laughed and yelled to each other as they jumped, sharing in the fun and excitement of doing something different.

Finally, the adult whales came behind at their regular slow pace. They broke the surface of the water to breathe then submerged again to swim through the water. They were swimming far ahead of their little ones, kicking their tailfins to move them forward. The adults were getting far ahead of their little ones as they plodded forward through the water.

Willy's mother called for him to return to the pod. Willy also heard the calls from other parents for their little ones to rejoin the pod. They all raced back to their parents, each trying to beat the other, diving over and bumping into each other as they swam.

Willy was not the first one back to his parents, but he swam up to his mother and rubbed up against her side. He was happy to be back. Willy liked having fun with the other young whales in their pod—they were his friends—but he always felt safer when he was with his parents because they loved him and took care of him and taught him how to find food, and how to stay out of danger.

Willy was happy when he was at home.

Willy Meets Humans

Willy was having a good day. He had found a big school of little fish and had a great breakfast. Then he saw two sharks and quickly returned to his parents. Even though he was a young whale, Willy knew that sharks would not attack a healthy pod of whales. But they would attack a young or old whale by himself if they thought they could get away with it.

Willy was swimming with his pod when they suddenly turned to the right. He did not know why they had turned, but he stayed with them. Before long, Willy saw two boats in the water. He had heard of boats before, but he had never seen one. He knew that another kind of animal called humans rode the backs of their boats and came out onto the water. These two boats were full of humans and they were all standing on the edge of their boat and staring at the pod of whales as they swam by.

Willy started to swim closer to the boat so he could have a better look at them. But his mother quickly guided him away from the boats and back to the pod. She did not want Willy to get hurt.

"Why can't I go closer," Willy asked. "I just want to see the humans up close."

"No, dear," said Willy's mother. "If you get too close, you might get hurt, or you might upset their boat. That would be terrible because humans cannot stay in the water for long like we can."

"If it's dangerous for them on the water," Willy began, "then why do they come on the water in their boats?"

"They want to know what it is like to live in water. They want to understand more about us, too." Willy's mother changed direction again to stay away from the two boats. Willy also changed direction to stay with his mother.

The pod kept swimming in a straight line for a long time. Then, they changed direction again. When Willy came up for a breath of air, he looked around to see why they had changed. "Whoa!" said Willy as he saw a very large boat coming toward his pod.

The pod changed direction again to stay away from the very large boat. The boat was white and had a lot of holes along the sides. Willy looked at it again as he swam past the very large boat. He saw more humans standing on the edge of the boat and watching the pod as it swam by. Some of them seemed to be waving their arms at the whales.

Willy stopped swimming and waved one of his fins at the humans. He heard a noise, like a bunch of humans yelling at the same time. It sounded like a happy noise. When it stopped, Willy waved his fin again and the noise started again. It sounded like they were cheering for him, but he had not done anything fancy or special. Willy was surprised at how easy it had been to please the humans, and because he did not understand them, he chose to obey his mother and stay away from the confusing humans.

Willy Learns to Sing

Willy woke up happy one morning. He was actually happy every morning, but this morning was something special. Today he would go on a long journey with his pod. The waters were getting cold and the pod always went where the water was warmer.

So Willy wanted to share his happiness with the rest of the pod so they could be happy too. Willy started to say something to his mother, but his words came out as a song. What was a song, you ask? Willy didn't know anything about singing or songs. He just wanted to tell them he was happy.

I feel good because we are going on a journey together.

On a journey together to warmer waters; warmer waters; warmer waters.

I feel good because we are a family and we are traveling together.

Together we travel and that makes me happy.

Willy's singing voice was high and still unsure of himself. But it was still a beautiful voice and many of the whales swimming nearby turned to look at this new voice and they smiled when saw it was the little one.

Willy's mother looked at her son and smiled. His song made her happy just listening to it. She nodded her head and let him know that she liked his song.

Mother kept swimming for a while. Then she turned and looked at her son.

I love my family and my son most of all.

My family gives me such great joy and happiness.

I love to swim with them and guide them to great places.

The waters of the ocean give us life and joy.

Mother's voice was beautiful. It was confident and strong and just listening to it made Willy feel even better. "Wow!," said Willy. Is that something we all can do?" he asked.

"Yes," Mother said with a happy laugh. "We all can do it, but I am surprised you have already learned to do it so well."

"Why? What do you mean?" Willy asked.

"Usually, whales don't learn to sing until they are nearly full grown. You're still a little one and yet you can sing as well as the greatest of the whales."

"Why do we sing?" asked Willy.

"We sing when we are happy and we sing when we are afraid. We sing when we are sad and we sing when we are full of joy," mother explained.

"Do we sing when we get angry?" Willy asked.

"Yes, dear, we sing especially when we get angry."

"Why?"

"Because anger makes us say and do things that hurt people—things that later we wish we had never said or done. So we sing to get rid of our anger and it helps us to be happy again."

Willy snuggled up against his mother's side as they swam. "I am going to sing a song every time I get angry," Willy promised his mother.

"That's good, dear," she replied. "If you can learn to control your anger, then you will be happier and you will have more friends and then they can also sing with you and everyone will be happy."

Funny Jokes

Q: What did the shark ask the whale?

A: What are you blubbering about?

Q: Why are fish so smart?

A: They are always in a school!

Q: What do you call a fish with no eyes?

A: FSH!

Q: Which fish go to heaven when they die?

A: Angelfish!

Q: What is a knight's favorite fish?

A: Swordfish!

Q: What did the fish say when he got out of jail?

A: I'm off the hook!

Q: What is a sea serpent's favorite meal?

A: Fish and ships!

Q: How did the fish's tail get stuck in the anchor?

A: It was just a fluke!

Q: What do whales chew?

A: Blubber gum!

Q: What do you call a deaf fishing boat captain?

A: Anything you like, because he can't hear you!

Q: What fish makes the best sandwiches?

A: The peanut butter and jellyfish!

Q: What do you call an infant whale?

A: A little squirt!

Q: Why are fish bad at tennis?

A: They don't like to get close to the net!

Maze 1

Maze 2

Maze 3

Maze 4

Maze 5

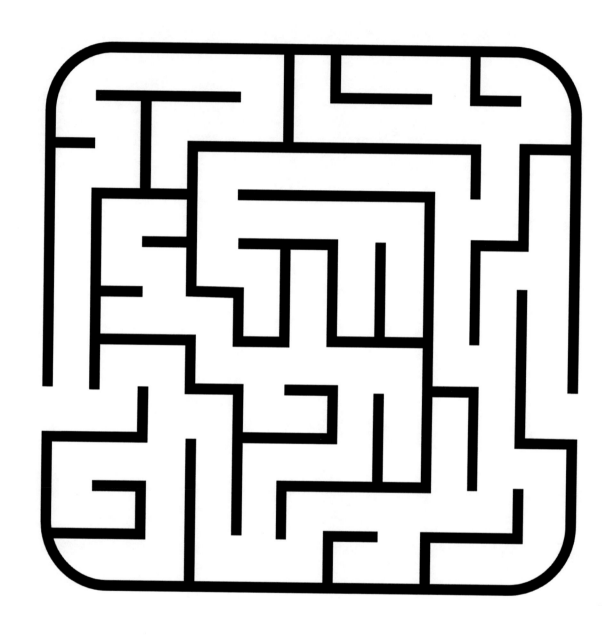

Solutions

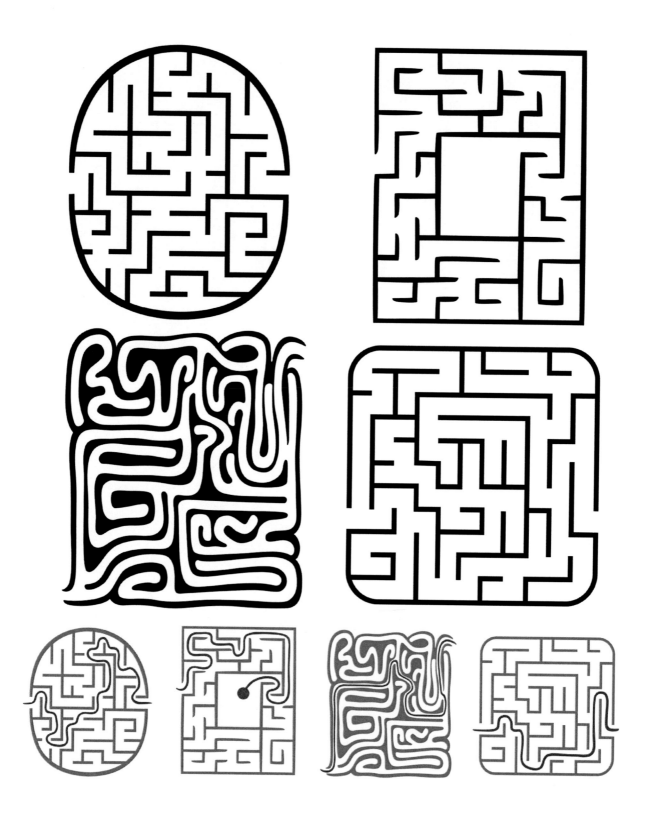

44092852R00015

Made in the USA
San Bernardino, CA
06 January 2017